Presented to:

_____

From:

_____

Date:

_____

THE
GREATEST
GIFT
EVER
GIVEN

Daniel R. Johnson

P.O. Box 882 • Kokomo, IN 46903-0882

The truths in this book surrounding the life and
ministry of Jesus Christ are factual. All other
characters are fictional.

THE GREATEST GIFT EVER GIVEN

published by Providence Publications

© 2001 by Daniel R. Johnson

International Standard Book Number: 0-9671383-5-3

Book and cover design by James W. Johnson

Printed in the United States of America

Scripture quotations are from the

King James Version (KJV).

For information:
PROVIDENCE PUBLICATIONS
P.O. Box 882 • Kokomo, IN 46903-0882

First printing 2001

With gratitude to . . .
the one who consistently
gave of herself to me—
placing my needs above
her own, preparing me for
life's opportunities, and
praying me through life's
difficulties—my mom.
I love you.

*A*re you sure? That was my first response to the question I had just been asked. It was the Friday after Thanksgiving and I was spending the afternoon ice skating with my cousin. Ashley is my uncle Jim's daughter, and since we have always been pretty close, I was happy to have the opportunity to spend some time with her.

While we took a break from skating and were drinking hot chocolate, Ashley saw her eighth grade homeroom teacher, Mrs. Davis. After a few minutes of small talk, Mrs. Davis asked me the unexpected question: "Julie, would you be willing to tell your story at our Winter Assembly?"

I was surprised because I was only a college junior and didn't see myself as much of a public speaker. In addition to that, the idea of standing in front of more than 100 junior high school students and saying something interesting or "assembly-worthy" scared me to death.

While talking together, I learned that Ashley had told Mrs. Davis quite a lot about me—especially about the rare and irreplaceable Christmas gift that I received in 1989 when I was only fourteen years old.

Ashley's version of the story had convinced Mrs. Davis that it was worth telling. In spite of my reluctance, Mrs. Davis turned out to be very persuasive, and I agreed to do it.

Ashley and I skated for a little while longer, but it was hard for me to concentrate as my mind kept racing back to those life-changing days in 1989.

As we walked home from the skating rink past several old houses that were already decorated for Christmas, Ashley and I reminisced about the story that I had been asked to share. Over the next couple of days as I was preparing for the assembly, I pored through scrapbooks, read my old diary, and shared several heart-to-heart conversations with my parents. It was a highly emotional journey back to the most traumatic season of my life.

The assembly was held on December 20, 1995. The school auditorium was full and I was as nervous as I had ever been. What I said that day ended up having quite an impact—not only on the audience—but also on me. Here is what I said:

Shortly after being discharged from the Union Army at the end of the Civil War, my great, great-grandfather and his new bride settled just a few miles down the road from where the school is now. Our family planted its roots even deeper in the area when my great-grandfather established Hillsboro's first lumber business in 1898.

Through five generations, two World Wars, and The Great Depression, our family has been proud to call Hillsboro "home." To this very day, my uncle Jim works on the family farm and my dad runs the lumberyard.

According to my brothers, when my parents learned that I was going to be born, they were less than excited about the prospect of having another child. I suppose Dad and Mom thought that three boys equaled a full house. The house was full, but when I came along, I added what I've always considered to be a des-

perately needed feminine flair to
our family.

My brothers, Brian, Jeff, and
Greg, all welcomed me into the
Porter family with open arms.
Boredom was never a problem for
me while growing up. When I
wasn't playing with the dolls that
my grandmother loved to buy me,
or riding horses at my uncle Jim's
farm, I was playing football or basketball with my brothers. I am
blessed to have a virtually endless
list of great childhood memories.

Even though the good times

were more enjoyable, without a doubt, I learned more from the tough times. One of those tough times was in fourth grade. That was the year when the old steel mill closed down, causing a lot of people to lose their jobs. It also caused a slowdown in business at the lumberyard.

Those were especially difficult days for my dad because, after generations of success, he was facing the possibility of failure. I can clearly remember how worried my parents became about paying the bills and keeping the lumberyard open.

In order to make it, they decided to sell our house and buy a less expensive one. It was common in those days to go to sleep at night listening to my dad's hammer as he worked to fix up the old house.

The difficulty of those experiences taught us that our relationships were more important than our possessions and that if we stuck together, we could survive the fiercest of challenges. In time, business at the lumberyard picked up.

When my brother, Brian (who is six years older than me), entered ninth grade, he started a new tradition for our family: playing high school basketball. For years, the team had been known for its mediocrity. But by the time Brian was a senior, they missed making the state tournament by only one game.

That was the beginning of our town's love affair with high school basketball. Once we had tasted victory, our appetite kept growing.

By the time my other brothers, Jeff and Greg were in high school, winning had become a full-fledged expectation.

In the fall of 1989, Jeff was a senior, Greg was a junior, and they were both in the starting lineup. Hopes around town were high about making it to the state tournament. I was a freshman that fall, trying to find my way in the shadow of my brothers' athletic success. I decided to join the cross-country team because, with three older brothers, running seemed natural to me.

Unfortunately, our season had barely begun when I came down with an upper respiratory infection, causing me to miss a couple weeks of practice and two meets. At the time, I thought it was just an ordinary illness, but it turned out to be far from ordinary.

On November 17th, after the cross-country season was over, I was getting ready to travel with my parents to a preseason basketball tournament in which Jeff and Greg were playing when I got sick again.

My mom thought about staying home with me, but I convinced her that I wasn't *that* sick, and so we went. By the time we got to the gym for the first game, I was having a hard time hiding how badly I felt. By halftime, I was having trouble breathing and I was getting scared.

As I fought to breathe, my dad found an usher who called 911. It was a little embarrassing to have everyone stare at me as the rescue team took me out on a stretcher, but I needed the help. For some

reason, my blood pressure was un-
usually low and yet my heart rate
was really high. The hospital that I
was taken to was one of the best
children's hospitals in the country.
Clearly, I was in the right place at
the right time.

Once in the emergency room,
doctors and nurses surrounded
me, hooked me up to all kinds of
monitors, and poked me with
more needles than I cared to
count. It was a pretty overwhelm-
ing experience.

While my brothers were win-

ning the preseason basketball tournament, I was beginning a busy
and frustrating journey from test
to test in an effort to discover why
I was so sick.

When the tournament was
over, Jeff and Greg—along with the
rest of the team—came to visit me
in the hospital. Wanting to cheer
me up, they had decided to give me
the net that they had cut down
from the goal after winning the final game. The net was nice, but it
was the gift that Jeff gave me that I
appreciated even more. It was a di-

ary. That diary became my closest friend in the hospital. In it, I was able to honestly express how I felt about what I was going through. For my first entry I wrote:

> *I've sensed for a while now that something isn't right inside me. I hoped that I was wrong but it looks like I was right. I'm only fourteen years old and I ought to be at home or out having fun with my friends instead of being in this hospital. It all feels like a bad dream and I'm*

ready to wake up!

A few days later a couple doctors came into my room to report the results of the tests. To put it simply, I flunked! The more they talked, the more frightened I became. They told me that I had a rare heart condition that at the time, I couldn't even pronounce or spell, but I have never forgotten it since.

What we thought had been a simple upper respiratory infection earlier that fall had in fact infected and severely damaged my heart. It was hard to understand everything that the doctors said, but it quickly became obvious that my condition was very serious.

As they talked, I was waiting to hear them describe what sort of medication or minor surgery would be needed to solve my problem. Unfortunately I didn't hear what I wanted to hear. The tests revealed that the left ventricle of my heart was no longer functioning. I didn't comprehend the significance of that fact until the doctor used a word that I never would have imagined hearing, not even in my worst nightmares: "transplant." (I can still hear my doctor's voice ringing in my ears as he said that I needed a new heart and I needed it soon!) When I realized that a heart transplant was my only chance for survival, all I could do was cry.

The idea of a heart transplant was shocking, confusing, and scary. Complicating matters, the doctors told us that my blood type, B negative, was extremely rare! My dad, who never cries, had to wipe tears from his eyes as he listened to the doctor and held onto both my mom and me.

That night, after my parents left, I wrote this in my diary:

The doctors came in this afternoon and took a sledge hammer to my dreams. I'd planned to go to college, get married, and have a family, but now all of that has been reduced from a solid plan to a far-fetched wish. I'm already tired of doctors and needles, I miss being home,

*and I'm getting sick of crying
myself to sleep at night. God,
if you're out there, why did
you let this happen?*

Over the next few weeks I received a crash course in cardiology—the study of the heart. I
learned about the process that
would lead to a transplant, the
challenges of locating a proper donor in time, and the risks of rejec-
tion following a transplant.

The bottom line was that I was
in a race that no fourteen-year-old
girl with a life full of hopes and

dreams would want to be in. It was a race between heart failure and a heart transplant.

To make matters even worse, all of this was happening in the middle of the holiday season. Decorations were everywhere, yet it was impossible for me to get into the Christmas spirit. I can re-member looking out my window one night at all of the Christmas lights. A shopping center nearby was crowded with happy and healthy people. It was hard to think about the world celebrating while I was dying.

On Christmas Eve, my parents and brothers all came to visit me in the hospital. Our family had always been together on Christmas Eve and we were determined not to allow my condition to ruin that record. We ate together and then opened a few Christmas presents. It felt good to be together, and for a few brief moments, I almost forgot I was in the hospital.

I fell asleep about nine o'clock that night but woke up a few hours later when the lights came on in my room. I was surprised to see my parents, my brothers and my doctor all come into the room. I was awake, but what they told me seemed like a dream: a possible donor, with type B negative blood, had been found!

It's hard to explain how I felt when I heard that news. It was a strange mixture of relief and fear. On the one hand, it was the chance at life for which I had been waiting. On the other hand, what if the heart didn't match? What if I didn't survive the surgery? What

if my body were to reject the new
heart?

As soon as they told me about
the potential match, everything
started to move very quickly. I
didn't have much time before I left
my room, but I did make one
more entry into my diary:

*Here we go. It's Christmas
Eve and something wonder-
ful is about to happen. At
least I hope so. I'm a little bit
excited and a whole lot
scared. Just in case I don't
wake up after surgery, Mom*

and Dad, I love you! You're the best parents a girl could have. I know that you never expected to have a fourth child and I'm sorry that the last month or so has been so hard for you, but thanks for giving me fourteen great years.

Brian, Jeff, and Greg, I love you so much! I can't imagine anyone being surrounded by a better support team than the three of you. Even though I didn't always

*enjoy it, thanks for making
me "one of the boys." If I
don't see you again, please
know that I'll love you forever.*

After writing that (and hoping
it wouldn't be the *last* thing I
would ever write), I was wheeled
out of my room to undergo a
couple last-minute tests. The doctors wanted to be sure that I was
strong enough for the operation
and that the donor heart was indeed a healthy match. Thankfully,
I was strong enough and the heart

was a match!

Just before surgery, I kissed everyone in my family good-bye. Then, after he asked me if I had any questions before the operation began, my surgeon leaned over and said, "Merry Christmas." Those were the last words that I remember hearing before I received the best Christmas gift of my life.

The operation itself lasted most of the night. Obviously, I don't remember any of it, although it was a long and restless night for my family. They were awake all night, anxiously awaiting the periodic reports from the operating room. Thankfully, the surgery went perfectly and I woke up the day after Christmas with a new heart. I was pretty groggy for the next few days, but I was amazed by how quickly I felt the benefit of my new heart.

The first time I wrote in my diary after the surgery, I said:

> *I'm alive!!! I used to take life for granted but I never will again. I'm weak and my*

*chest hurts, but for the first
time in over a month, I'm
excited about the future.*

Just ten days after the surgery I
went home from the hospital. As I
healed, my greatest concern was
whether or not my body would reject the new heart. On January
14th, I thought my worst fears
were turning into reality when I
was rushed back to the clinic with
a fever. Fortunately, the doctors
were able to get it under control
by fine tuning my medication.
Steadily, I regained strength.

Believe it or not, I got really excited when two of my teachers started tutoring me a couple days each week to help me catch up on my schoolwork. What felt good was getting back to a normal life—or at least as normal a life as a fourteen-year-old girl with a heart transplant could have.

What also lifted my spirits during that winter was the fact that our high school basketball team was on a roll. Everybody in town was hoping for a state championship and the team seemed to be unstoppable. Because I wasn't strong enough to go to any of the games, Mom and Dad videotaped them so I could watch them at home.

I loved watching the games, partly because earlier in the season, while I was in the hospital waiting for the transplant, the team had decided to dedicate their season to me. As a symbol of their dedication, after each timeout and before every free throw, the players would tap their chests—right over their hearts—as their way of saying, "This is for Julie." I don't

know how many people knew
what they were doing, but it sure
meant a lot to me.

The team's winning streak continued right into the month of
March and the state championship
tournament. For the first time in
our town's history, our high school
basketball team was playing for
the state title. It was a huge deal!
Dad went to the game, while
Mom and I stayed at home and
watched it on TV.

It was one of the closest and
best games of the season. We

ended up winning by four points.

After the game, as the majority of Hillsboro was celebrating in the stands, the TV announcer interviewed some of the players. When he came to my brother Jeff, who was the team's captain, I could hardly believe what I heard. Jeff said, "Two and a half months ago, my little sister underwent heart transplant surgery. She couldn't be here, but I know she's watching at home tonight. I want everybody to know that her strength and courage have motivated and inspired us through every game this season. Thanks, Julie, for your great example. This one's for you!" After Jeff said that, everyone on the team tapped his chest one last time.

Without question, that was a championship season for all of us. Sitting at home that night and watching the team celebrate, I realized that I wasn't a *victim,* but a *victor,* having won a tough battle against a strong opponent. We all learned that year to overcome obstacles with the support and encouragement of our teammates.

We learned to be courageous. We also learned to refuse to give up until the final victory was won.

In so many ways, what began as the worst season of my life ended as the best season of my life. I wouldn't want to repeat those events, but what I learned from them has greatly enriched my life. I am convinced that everyone needs to learn the lessons I learned that year. When you face life's challenges, don't run from them, but learn from them!

At the close of my speech, the school principal asked the students if they wanted to ask me any questions. Little did I know that the very first question would lead me into yet another exciting season of life. It was simply, "Whose heart do you have?" I answered by admitting that I didn't know the donor's name, only that it had come from a thirteen-year-old boy. I answered a few more questions, but it was the one about the donor that kept bouncing back and forth in my mind.

A few weeks later my curiosity about that thirteen-year-old boy became too strong to ignore any longer. I decided to try to find the family who had given me such an extraordinary Christmas gift. Not knowing how else to locate them, I called the office of the doctor who had performed the transplant surgery. The person I spoke to wasn't able to release the family's name. That didn't surprise me, but I was pleased when she agreed to contact the family on my behalf.

I can still remember that it was

January 27 when I found a letter
in my mailbox. The letter was
from Susan Winston, a name I
didn't recognize. At first, I thought
the envelope may have been deliv-
ered to the wrong "Julie Porter,"
but I went ahead and opened it.
What I found was a letter from
the mother of the thirteen-year-
old boy whose heart was now
mine. Her words were incredibly
moving.

> *Dear Julie,*
>
> *My name is Susan Winston.*
> *Someone in Dr. Simpson's office*

*at Children's Hospital called
our home a few weeks ago and
said that you wanted to get in
touch with us. At first I wasn't
sure if I wanted to contact you,
but the more my husband,
Mike, and I talked about it,
the more we believed that it
was a good idea.*

*Our son, John, died on
Christmas Eve 1989. I don't
think we will ever completely get
over our loss, but it does bring us
great relief to know that his
heart is still beating in you, and*

that you are doing well.

John was the younger of our two boys. Like a lot of boys, he loved playing basketball and Little League baseball. In the fall of 1989 he was in eighth grade, busy having fun with his friends and trying to get along with his older brother, Brad.

The Christmas season that year seemed pretty ordinary until Christmas Eve, when we went to John's grandparents' house for dinner. On the way to their house—when we were just

a few miles from their home—
someone who had been drinking ran a stop sign and hit us
broadside. In an instant and
without warning, our quiet
ride turned into chaos.

The greatest impact was in
the back seat where John was sitting. Brad was only slightly in-
jured and Mike and I were both
all right. John wasn't so fortu-
nate. I'll never forget calling out
to him, asking if he was all
right, and not getting an answer. He was unconscious and

we couldn't tell what was wrong.

When the fire trucks and ambulances arrived, the paramedics quickly removed John from the car. It was getting dark and I couldn't see what all they were doing, but it was obvious that he was seriously hurt. When they told us they wanted to transport him to the hospital by helicopter, we knew that it was even worse than we had initially feared.

We got to the hospital about forty minutes after John. Seeing him in the emergency room with all the tubes and machines hooked up to his precious body was almost more than we could bear. Our boy, who had been so excited about Christmas just an hour earlier, was now fighting for his life. John's most serious injury was to his head. I can't remember how long we waited before a group of doctors, including a neurologist, led us into a small consultation room. They told us that John had suffered a severe brain injury and

*that his chances for survival
were not very good.*

*After conducting several more
tests, the doctors met with us
again to tell us that the scans of
John's brain confirmed their
fears: there was no brain activ-
ity. Though the doctors didn't
exactly say it, we knew that
John was gone. The only thing
keeping his body alive was the
life support machines.*

*To say that the news was
hard to take is an understate-
ment. Mike, Brad, and I cried*

like we had never cried before.
We held onto each other while
praying and trying to figure out
what to do. After giving us
some time together, one of the
doctors returned to talk with us
about various options, includ-
ing donating John's organs. It
was difficult to hear and even
more difficult to consider doing,
but we knew it was the right
thing to do, so we agreed.
Thankfully, during those long
and dark hours, God gave us
the power and peace to endure

*the worst pain that we have
ever experienced.*

*When Dr. Simpson's office
called a few weeks ago, all the
memories of John's final hours
rushed back to the surface
again. At the same time, the
call also sparked our "on again/
off again" curiosity about the
recipient of John's heart. We're
glad that you tried to reach us.
If you really want to, we are
ready to meet you.*

Sincerely,

Sue Winston

By the time I finished reading the letter, my hands were shaking and tears were clouding my eyes. I was more eager than ever to meet this family to whom I felt connected, even though we had never met. That evening I called the phone number that Mrs. Winston had written at the bottom of her letter. Our phone conversation was a little awkward at first and yet the longer we talked, the easier it became.

After several phone calls and a few more letters, Sue Winston and

I were becoming friends. We finally decided to get together and meet one another face-to-face during my Spring Break.

The Winstons lived in a nice community about an hour from my hometown, where Sue's husband, Mike, was a dentist. When I arrived, Mike, Sue, and their son, Brad, were all at home. At first I was a little afraid that my presence might be a gloomy reminder of John's death. Instead, they insisted that I reminded them of John's *life*. I felt at home.

Over the next several months I became increasingly close to John's family. We regularly talked on the phone, exchanged letters, and occasionally got together.

As Christmas approached (now seven years after John's life and mine were uniquely connected), Brad called and invited me to spend Christmas Eve with them. In keeping with their family's tradition, we had dinner at Dr. Winston's parents' home, where I met John's entire family. Once again they caused me to feel as if I belonged with them. The evening was a lot of fun, although it was impossible not to think about the Christmas Eve when all of our lives had been so dramatically changed.

By the time we got back to the Winston's house, we were fighting back tears while thinking and talking about John. Since it was getting late and snow was falling, I accepted their invitation to spend the night.

While sitting around the Christmas tree, I thanked them

again for meeting the greatest
need that I ever had with the
greatest gift that I had ever been
given. As we talked, Mike began
to tell the story of an even greater
Christmas gift.

He started the story by telling
me about John's birth. Brad was
just a little more than a year old
when they learned that John was
on the way. For nine long months
their excitement built until Febru-
ary 13, 1976, when John was born
at 10:42 P.M. He weighed eight
pounds three ounces. Everyone

was thrilled when they saw and held him for the first time. Sue was also greatly relieved, having endured nearly seven hours of labor.

During those late night hours, none of them could have imagined what the future held and what a rare gift John would eventually give to a little one-year-old girl who was sound asleep in her bed just 65 miles away. At that time, Mike and Sue could see John only as God's gift *to them*.

"Similar to our story of John's

birth," Mike continued, "two thousand years ago there lived a simple young girl named Mary who learned that she would soon give birth to a son."

Once Mike said that, I realized that the gift he was telling me about wasn't just any gift; He was Jesus, the greatest gift ever given.

Mike told me that Mary lived an average life in the little Jewish town of Nazareth, where the most exciting part of her life was her engagement to a carpenter named Joseph. There was nothing unusual or extraordinary about either Joseph or Mary—that is, until the angel Gabriel appeared.

When Gabriel first appeared to Mary, he said, "Thou hast found favour with God. And behold, thou shalt conceive in thy womb, and bring forth a son, and shalt call his name JESUS" (Luke 1:30, 31).

Being a virgin, Mary must have been stunned and confused by the angelic prediction. Why was she favored in God's eyes? Why had she been selected to give

birth to such a special child?
Gabriel's words must have echoed
in Mary's ears for days as she tried
to accept the idea of being part of
the most incredible miracle of all
time.

The Son of the living God was
to be supernaturally placed—in
embryonic form—inside her
womb. She would carry Him for
nine of the most amazing months
of history. She would be His
mother and He would be her Son.

Mary probably felt the widest
range of emotions that any human

being ever experienced. The Son of God was to be her child! As this amazing truth sank into Mary's mind, she was confronted with the nearly impossible task of telling her family and friends. What would they think? Her story surely sounded like the most outlandish tale anyone had ever heard.

Thankfully, Gabriel told Joseph about the miracle—as well as the importance of keeping his commitment to Mary. He stayed by her side every step of the way.

As Mary's due date approached, what appeared to be a horrible coincidence of timing occured: the Roman government announced a census. In those days, the census required everyone to return to his hometown to register. For Joseph and Mary, that meant traveling to the tiny little village of Bethlehem. To make matters worse, when they arrived in Bethlehem, there was no place to stay. Their only option was to spend the night in a barn.

Late in the evening, Joseph and Mary were awakened by the

bright light of glory. The time had come. Jesus was about to arrive. Joseph and Mary would soon have the unparalleled privilege of doing what no human being had ever done before: to touch the very face of God!

There was no obstetrician in Bethlehem's barn, no surgical gowns, no sterile instruments, no anesthetic. Joseph probably cut the umbilical cord and then he and Mary heard the voice of God. What a moment! Jesus was born!

The birth announcement read:

"For unto you is born this day in the city of David a Saviour, which is Christ the Lord" (Luke 2:11).

In spite of the less than glorious environment, it was indeed a glorious event. Unlike most such occasions, no friends or relatives came to celebrate Jesus' arrival. Instead, a group of angels shared their congratulations from the sky, and a band of nearby shepherds, sensing a holy event, came to see the precious baby.

As Mary drifted off to sleep on that remarkable night, she must have been overwhelmed by her blessed role. That night she began the most exciting relationship that any human being could ever experience. She would have the unique privilege of caring for, feeding, snuggling, holding, teaching, and later learning from Jesus. What she didn't fully comprehend on that first Christmas so many years ago, was what a rare and irreplaceable gift Jesus would become.

As Mike told me the old familiar Christmas story, it brought back memories of my childhood when my parents took me to a little church where I heard the story of Joseph and Mary and baby Jesus. I had always enjoyed the story, but up until that night around the Winston's Christmas tree it was only that—a story.

However, as I listened to it that night, I began to realize that the story of Jesus' birth was not just about a *baby* being born, but a *gift* being given.

As we continued to talk, Sue asked me what it was like when I was in the hospital waiting for a heart to become available. I told her how slowly the clock seemed to move and how full of worry I was as I wondered whether I would live or die. Even more frustrating was my inability to do anything about my condition. I was helpless to overcome the damage that the virus had caused to my heart.

"Almost like that," Mike said, "Jesus was born at a time when the whole world was waiting for a cure for the spiritual disease called sin."

In a manner eerily similar to

the way in which a virus had invaded and damaged my heart, sin had invaded the lives of everyone on earth—including mine. When Mike suggested that I was sinful, I didn't have a problem agreeing with him. What I *did* have a problem accepting though was the idea that my efforts to lead a moral life were not enough to overcome my sin.

Noticing my reluctance to view myself as being in "critical condition" spiritually, Mike showed me a verse in his Bible. It said, "For the wages of sin is death; but the gift of God is eternal life through Jesus Christ our Lord" (Romans 6:23).

When I heard that verse, it made me feel kind of like I did when my doctor had explained my need of a transplant. I hadn't wanted it to be true, but somehow—deep down inside—I knew that it was true. Just as I couldn't overcome my fatal heart condition on my own, I couldn't overcome the fatal consequences of sin on my own. I needed the rarest and most irreplaceable gift imaginable. I needed Jesus.

In the glow of the Christmas lights, I finally understood the most important lesson of my life: *when genuine love sees a great need, it gives a great gift.* In a way, I had already experienced that truth, but that night it took on new significance.

Mike explained that my frustrating wait for a new heart came to an end only because of a monumentally painful event. Mike's voice cracked a bit as he talked about the accident. As Sue had done in her first letter to me, he mentioned the devastating feeling of calling out to John and not receiving an answer. Mike wasn't able to hold back the tears when he told me about holding John's lifeless body in the emergency room. "It was late that night" he said, "when we agreed to donate John's heart, enabling him to save your life."

Similarly, the world's long and frustrating wait for a chance at new life also came to an end because of a monumentally painful event. Just as my diseased heart needed to be removed and John's healthy heart put in its place, my sin needed to be removed and Jesus needed to fill the void. In order for that to happen, Jesus had to die.

Jesus' death was not an accident and it didn't occur in a sterile hospital, but at a place called Calvary. Calvary was a gruesome spot next to a trash heap. There, Jesus' hands and feet were nailed to a splintery wooden cross in between a couple of hardened and condemned criminals.

Standing just a few feet away from the horror of the cross was Mary, Jesus' mother. From the day she had given birth to Him in the barn in Bethlehem, until that dark day at Calvary, Mary had never stopped loving, never stopped caring, and never stopped dreaming for her Son. Yes, she knew that He had a divine mission to accomplish, yet the pain that she felt watching her Son die must have been excruciating.

After Jesus died, Mary grieved

for three long days and sleepless nights. But then a miracle that no medical team could duplicate occurred: Jesus rose from the dead! On the Sunday morning after His death, the tomb in which He had been placed was empty and Jesus was alive. He had proven, once and for all, that He had power over death and the ability to remove the disease of sin.

"In order to receive John's heart," Mike explained, "you had to endure a long and dangerous operation. But to receive God's gift of Jesus, all you have to do is believe."

Sue still had her Bible open, so she read another verse to me. I had heard it before, but this time I understood its true meaning. The verse was John 3:16, which says, "For God so loved the world, that he gave his only begotten Son, that whosoever believeth in him should not perish, but have everlasting life."

By the time Sue finished reading the verse, I was beginning to feel a lot like I had seven years earlier when the light came on in my hospital room and I learned that a heart was available. This time, a light had come on in my soul, causing me to realize that I needed what only God could give: Jesus Christ.

And so that night, while we all held hands, I prayed a very simple prayer asking God to forgive my sin and grant me eternal life. With tears in our eyes, we hugged as I thanked them all for not only telling me about God, but for *showing* me God's love.

Just as I will be forever grateful
to the Winstons for giving me John's
heart, I will also be forever grateful
to God for giving me Jesus. I'll never
forget that night when God met the
greatest need I ever had with the
greatest gift ever given.

I've lost track now of how many
times I've told the story of my two
remarkable Christmases. Finally, after a lot of encouragement, and a
little pushing, I've agreed to write it
all down.

It's been ten years since my lifesaving transplant surgery and three years since my life-changing choice to receive Jesus. Over the past few years I've told my parents and brothers on several occasions about God's gift, and I think they're close to accepting it.

I have also continued to be close to John's family—especially Brad. It wasn't long after I believed in Jesus that our friendship flourished into a romance. We were married a year and a half ago.

I'm finishing this while waiting for the entire Porter and Winston families to arrive for Christmas dinner. I'm not much of a cook and it's been kind of a hectic day, but I think I'm ready for them.

It's been busy in part because I spent most of my morning at the hospital. No, I'm not sick. I went to the hospital because I am a nurse in the pediatric cardiology unit at Children's Hospital. That's right, *I work at the very same Children's Hospital where I got my new heart ten years ago.* I suppose all those days I spent as a patient burdened me to give back to others who are in need.

Actually, I didn't *have* to go to the hospital this morning—I *wanted* to go. I wanted to visit and wish my patients a Merry Christmas, because I know how difficult it is to be in the hospital on Christmas.

I took Ashley, now seventeen, with me so that I could once again tell her the story of Jesus, the greatest gift ever given. I am hoping and praying that this will become another life-changing Christmas to remember!

HOW TO BECOME A CHRISTIAN

THE BIBLE DESCRIBES three key steps in becoming a Christian.

I MUST:

1

ADMIT that I am a sinner, unable to live up to God's standard of perfection and, therefore, am deserving of eternal separation from God.

"For all have sinned, and come short of the glory of God" (Romans 3:23).

"For the wages of sin is death; but the gift of God is eternal life through Jesus Christ our Lord" (Romans 6:23).

2 ACKNOWLEDGE that Jesus is God's only Son, Who died on the cross to pay the penalty for my

sin. He arose from the grave three days later in victory over death.

"But God commendeth his love toward us, in that, while we were yet sinners, Christ died for us"
(Romans 5:8).

"Christ died for our sins according to the scriptures; . . .he was was buried, and . . .rose again the third day according to the scriptures"
(1 Corinthians 15:3, 4).

3 BELIEVE in Jesus Christ alone for the forgiveness of my sins and for the gift of eternal life in heaven.

"For God so loved the world, that he gave his only begotten Son, that whosoever believeth in him should not perish, but have everlasting life" (John 3:16).

"For whosoever shall call upon the name of the Lord shall be saved" (Romans 10:13).

IF YOU ARE READY to become a Christian, honestly believing each of these three statements to be true, then pray from your heart the following prayer:

"God in Heaven, I know that I am a sinner, and I understand that my sin deserves to be severely punished. I believe that because of Your love,

*Jesus took my punish-
ment when He died
on the cross. Please
forgive me of my sin
and give me the gift
of eternal life. Thank
You for hearing my
prayer and receiving
me into Your family.*

Amen."

WELCOME to God's family! Please quickly contact a trusted Christian friend or church, and tell them about your belief in Christ.

P.O. Box 882 • Kokomo, IN 46903-0882

ABOUT THE AUTHOR
DANIEL JOHNSON has pastored local churches in Illinois and Indiana. He currently ministers in Kokomo, Indiana, where he resides with his wife, Linda, and their four children.

ARE THESE PROVIDENCE PUBLICATIONS IN YOUR LIBRARY?

THE GREATEST SOLDIER WHO EVER LIVED

This is a story of liberation told in a fresh, new way. *The Greatest Soldier Who Ever Lived* is a poignant and powerful parable of family, faith, and freedom. It will undoubtedly touch your heart. And it may even change your life—forever!

THE GREATEST FATHER WHO EVER LIVED

Every father needs a wise example to follow. *The Greatest Father Who Ever Lived* is an exciting and emotionally-charged parable that tells the story of a father's love, a son's courage, and the legacy that they leave. It will no doubt inspire men everywhere to rise to the challenge of fatherhood.

THE TEACHER'S DAILY HELPER

This year-long devotional guide is structured around 52 teaching themes. *The Teacher's Daily Helper* is designed so that in two to five minutes a day, through the disciplines of prayer and meditation, a teacher will be encouraged to focus on God.